A NOTE ABOUT THE MANUFACTURING OF THIS BOOK

This book has been printed on Forest Stewardship Council® certified paper.
The FSC®'s mission is to promote environmentally sound, socially beneficial,
and economically prosperous management of the world's forests.

All Kalaniot Books have accompanying activity guides.
Download them for free at KalaniotBooks.com.

Text copyright © by The Hebrew University Magnes Press
and The Seymour Fox School of Education, The Hebrew University of Jerusalem
Text by Haya Shenhav
Illustrations copyright © by Yirmi Pinkus
English translation copyright © by The Hebrew University Magnes Press and
The Seymour Fox School of Education, The Hebrew University of Jerusalem
Translated to English by Gilah Kahn-Hoffmann
Published by arrangement with the Cohen Shiloh Literary Agency

First American edition published 2024 by Kalaniot Books,
an imprint of Endless Mountains Publishing Company
72 Glenmaura National Boulevard, Suite 104B, Moosic, Pennsylvania 18507
www.KalaniotBooks.com

Library of Congress Control Number: 2023943442
ISBN: 978-1-962011-99-0
Printed in the United States of America
First Printing

100 ROOMS

WRITTEN BY
HAYA SHENHAV

ILLUSTRATED BY
YIRMI PINKUS

TRANSLATED BY
GILAH KAHN-HOFFMANN

Kalaniot Books
Moosic, Pennsylvania

ONCE there was a man who wanted a house. He called the builders and said to them, "Build me a house." And the builders built him a small house.

"Bigger," he told them. "Add a room."
And the builders added a room.
"Bigger," he told them. "Add another room."
And the builders added another room.
"And another," the man said. And the
builders added another room, and another,
and more and more rooms.

And the small house became a big house, a huge house, a gigantic house. As if it were a palace. As if the man were a king. But the man wasn't a king. He was just a man. He didn't have a crown and he didn't have servants. He didn't have horses and he didn't have chariots. He didn't have ministers and he didn't have a kingdom. He was just a man.

When the builders finished building the house, the man counted the rooms: 1 ... 2 ... 3 ... 4 ... 5 ... 10 ... 20 ... 30 ... 40 ... 50 ... 60 ... 70 ... 80 ... 90 ... 100! 100 rooms!

Wonderful, wonderful! thought the man. *A house like this is exactly what I need!* And he started to put things away. In one room he put chairs, and in another he put tables.

He put books in one room, and in another he hung pictures. He put plates in one room and forks in another. In one room he put beds, and in another he hung curtains.

When he reached the last room, the 100th room, he had nothing left to put there. *This will be an empty room,* thought the man, and he closed the door.

He was tired and hungry. *Now I will eat something, and after that I will go to sleep.*

The man went into the room with the plates and took a plate.

Next, he went into the room with the forks and took a fork.

And then he went into the room with the food, and helped himself to a big portion.

He went into the room with the tables and put his food on a table.

He wanted to sit down and eat, but the chairs were in another room. He was so tired and hungry that he simply sat down on the floor and ate.

After that he decided to go to sleep. He went into the room with the beds to lie down. But the light coming through the window disturbed him. He wanted to draw the curtains, but they were in a different room. He went into the room with the curtains and drew them all. And then he went back to the room with the beds and lay down. But of course the light coming through the window still disturbed him. He covered his head with his blanket and fell asleep.

The next morning, the man woke up
and wanted to put on clean clothes. But
he couldn't remember where his clothes
were. Maybe they were in room 10? In
room 10 he found his brooms. Maybe
they were in room 20? He went to room
20 and found his baskets. Maybe they
were in room 50? He went to room 50
where he found a plant.

Maybe his clothes were in room 80? In room 80 he found a mirror.

He looked in the mirror and saw a dirty, tired, and frustrated man. *What should I do?* he thought. *I can't find anything. This house is too big for me.*

And then he looked out the window and
saw the woods and heard birds chirping.
Suddenly he knew what he had to do.

The man went from room to room and gathered up the things he needed: a chair and a table, a bed and a cupboard, some plates, some pots and pans, some food, some books, and a few more things—and he put them all in the empty room, the 100th room.

He stayed in that room and he was happy.

The next day, the man placed an ad in the newspaper: 99 ROOMS FOR SALE. THE ROOMS ARE BIG AND THE PRICES ARE LOW!

People read the ad and came and bought the rooms.

After the man had sold all the rooms, he bought himself a hat. Now every morning, he puts on his hat and goes for a walk in the woods. On the way he meets his neighbors. "Good morning," he greets them.

And the neighbors answer joyfully, "Good morning to you!"

In **100 ROOMS**, our hero struggles with his many possessions. When he sells his rooms (at a low price!), not only is he happier, but others benefit from his generosity. Finally without the distraction of "stuff," he is able to create friendships with his neighbors.

In their collection of writings on ethics, the ancient Jews advised "The more possessions, the more worry," (Pirkei Avot, Chapter 2, Mishna 8). When we have many possessions, we may worry that our things will be damaged. We may worry that they will be taken away. We may even worry that we don't have enough things to make us happy. But the reality is that it is not our possessions, but our connections with other people, that truly make us happy.